W9-AYC-217

For Jaycee, Joshua, and Alec

Coyote.

Blue Coyote.
He was going along, following his nose.
He had a nose for trouble.

Coyote stuck his nose into Badger's hole but got bitten.

Coyote wanted to have a flaming red head like Woodpecker, but his fur caught fire.

Coyote went looking for Snake
but only found trouble.

Coyote was always in trouble.

Coyote came to a place where
earth meets sky.
He heard laughing and singing.
He went up to take a look.

Coyote saw a flock of crows.
They were chanting.
They were dancing.

Then the birds spread their wings.
They flew through the air and circled the canyon.

"Oh, if only I could fly," said Coyote. "I would be the greatest coyote in all the world!"

Coyote called to the crows.
"Let me join you," he said.

"This foolish coyote wants to be like us,"
Old Man Crow said to his flock.
"Let's have some fun with him."

Old Man Crow turned one eye toward Coyote. "You may dance with us," he said.

"Thank you! Thank you!" said Coyote. "But I want to fly, too!"

"Maybe you can," said Old Man Crow.

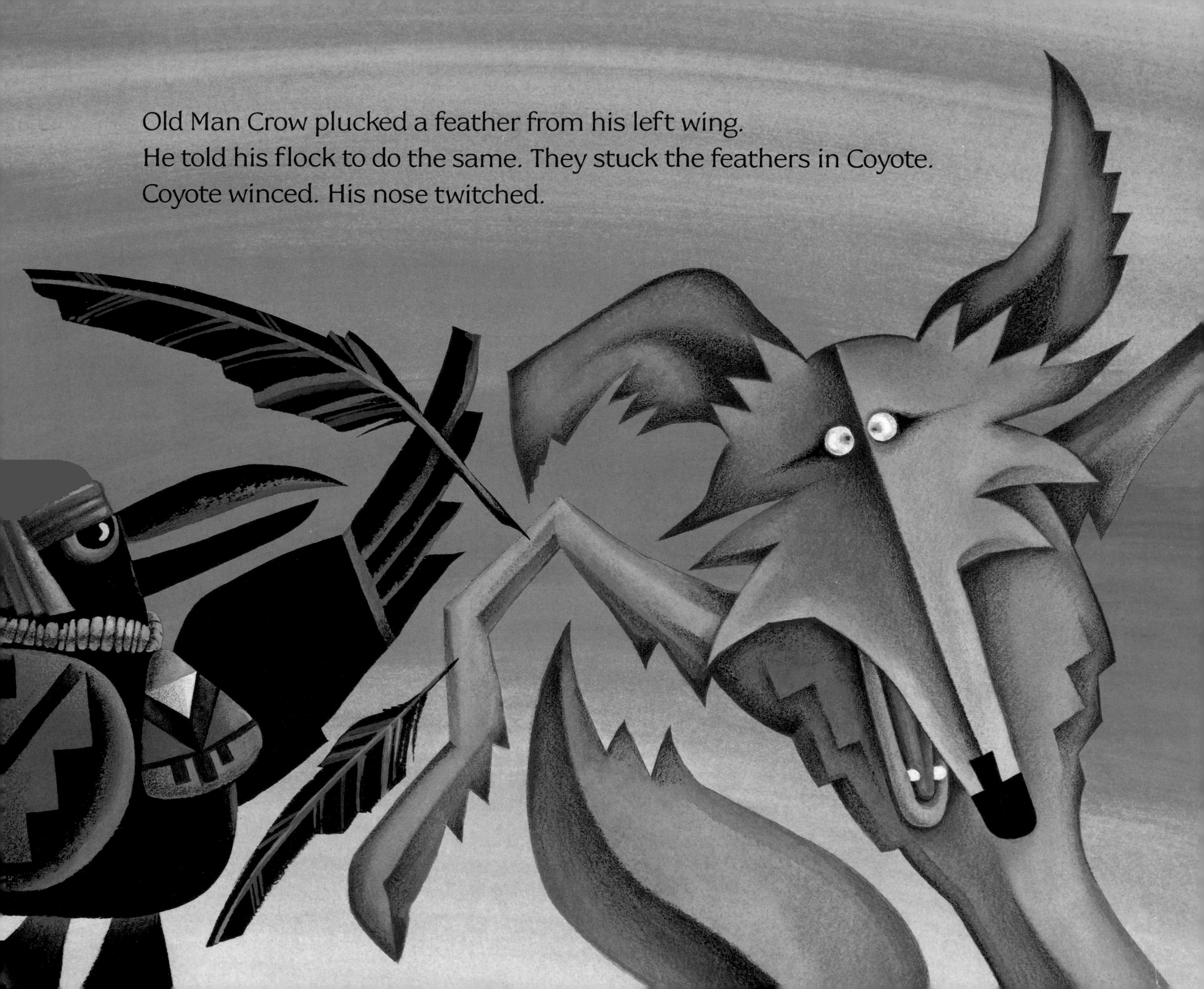

Old Man Crow plucked a feather from his left wing.
He told his flock to do the same. They stuck the feathers in Coyote.
Coyote winced. His nose twitched.

The crows chuckled.

"You are ready to fly," said Old Man Crow.

The birds began their slow, steady chant. They hopped from one foot to the other. Coyote joined in the dance. Even though he got out of step and sang out of tune, he was very proud of himself.

The crows spread their wings and soared into the sky. Coyote followed. His flight was jerky. He tilted to one side. Since his feathers were only from the left wing of each bird, he was off balance.

He fell to the ground.
"Wait!" he cried out.
"Don't leave me behind!"

The birds returned and gathered round Coyote.
"We must balance him," said Old Man Crow.

Old Man Crow plucked a feather from his *right* wing. Each of his flock did the same. Coyote cringed as they stuck the feathers in his fur. The crows cackled.

"Now I'm perfect!" said Coyote. "I can fly as well as the rest of you."

Coyote had become rude and boastful.
He danced out of step.
He sang off-key.
The crows were no longer having fun.

The birds again began their slow, steady chant.
Coyote hopped along, flapping his feathered legs and
singing sour notes.
The dancers spread their wings and leapt into the air.

Soon the crows were flying high over the canyon.
Coyote struggled to keep up.

"Carry me!" he demanded.

The crows circled Coyote but didn't carry him.
Instead, they took back their feathers, one by one.

Coyote sank through the air.

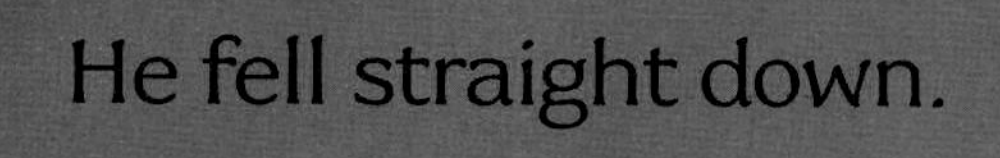

He fell straight down.

“Woooooooooooo!” he howled.

Coyote fell so fast, his tail caught fire.
He fell into a pool on the mesa.

Coyote crawled out of the water.
He heard laughter and saw the crows flying away.